Smell

Of

The Dead

Dale Eldon

A CIP catalogue record for this book
is available from the British Library

ISBN 978-0-9576480-1-2

Printed and bound in Great Britain
Crowded Quarantine Publications
34 Cheviot Road
Wolverhampton
West Midlands
WV2 2HD

© Crowded Quarantine Publications 2013
www.crowdedquarantine.co.uk

ALSO BY DALE ELDON

SHORT STORIES:

Potato Man, found in the anthology, GRINDHOUSE*.

Mr. Cuddles, found in the anthology, CARNIVAL OF THE DAMNED.

Daughter's Prey, found in the anthology, I'LL NEVER GO AWAY VOL 2.

Shatter, found in the drabble anthology, LITTLE TALES FOR THE SMALLEST ROOM.

My short story, DARK DWELLINGS

*Crowded Quarantine Publications

Dedication

To all those who helped make this story possible:

The Millard Clan at Crowded Quarantine Publications - thank you so much for picking up SMELL OF THE DEAD. To my friend Rebecca Besser who inspired me to check into CQ, and her continued friendship. To my most wonderful friend, Gregory L. Norris, a person who belongs in the hall of fame for authors, and the best friend a person could ask for - thank you for your undying support.

To my mother, who gave me the idea of the zombie plague which is based on real diseases and viruses. Thank you for everything. Thank you, Jordyn Redwood, for your medical expertise in further development of the virus. To my uncle John Szewczyk (Sev-Check), who not only inspired me to go back to my zombies on a mountain idea, but helped me to learn more about Everest. And thank you dad, for passing the desire to write onto me.

For the people who wished that I fail, you too have been a HUGE inspiration. Whether you wanted it, or not, you were the kick in the rear I needed to continue writing.

The law of Mount Everest is, you stay where you die...

"But we were born of risen apes, not fallen angels, and the apes were armed killers besides. And so what shall we wonder at? Our murders and massacres and missiles, and our irreconcilable regiments? Or our treaties whatever they may be worth; our symphonies however seldom they may be played; our peaceful acres, however frequently they may be converted into battlefields; our dreams however rarely they may be accomplished. The miracle of man is not how far he has sunk but how magnificently he has risen. We are known among the stars by our poems, not our corpses."

— **Robert Ardrey**

Chapter One

Why didn't you jump? Fucking coward. Staring deep into his metal camping mirror, Doctor Terry Marshall pondered. Behind his glazed, dark blue eyes, his mind moved to seeing himself standing on the other side of the guard rail on a bridge, the wind whipping and straddling his clothes, his car left parked cockeyed with the driver's side door hanging open. During the morning time, the bridge was vacant, no audience to watch him fall to his death. No one to stop him, except...

Terry's mind could be such a bastard, always interjecting at the worst possible moment. He tried urging himself to jump, but his conscience urged him in the opposite direction. That nagging voice made ex-wives seem quiet.

In those days, all hope abandoned Terry. The face of front page science magazines around the world, the forty-year-old who looked thirty, the world renowned DNA sequencer who had made an astonishing breakthrough, now declared dead.

Sitting in his yellow, three-man-mountain tent, he tired of staring at the mirror. Facing the man responsible for the safety of his friends, if he couldn't look at himself, Terry might as well give up. Alive or not, anticipation vexed him. His eyes screamed words that were almost audible in his head: *You need to stop thinking about the past, and concentrate on the now.*

His face became sore once he'd scratched the same spot for almost an hour. He fastened his boot straps and crawled out of his tent. The tranquil bliss of the sun radiated over his body, empowering him. He sucked in the thin mountain air while standing at Advanced Base Camp (ABC) of Mount Everest.

"Still getting use to the altitude?" Doctor Ronald Kane asked from his stoop at the entrance of his tent.

Well, if it's not my favorite prick. Terry thought.

"Naw, this isn't anything to sneeze at, and it's not my first time." Terry gave a wink.

"That's right, you climbed K2?" Kane stood up and stretched his arms.

Terry nodded as he panned over the site for the rest of his group.

"Damn, after a hard climb like that, this rock must be a cake-walk." Kane trotted over to Terry. "You summit too, didn't you?"

"Barely. What's that pack?" Terry pointed with his chin, glancing inside Kane's tent.

"The gray one by my bunk?"

"Yeah."

"That's my paraglider, my plan to safely get off this rock once I summit," Kane said, cracking knuckles.

"Where the hell do you plan landing with that thing?"

"The town of Namche Bazaar, within an hour of summiting. It's going to be an intoxicating view."

"But the way up is only half of the climb," Terry said with an arched eyebrow.

"The descent also has the highest death rate. I don't plan on dying up here. Well, Ter, I'm off. Try not to freeze to death."

The moment Kane left Terry's sight, he dropped his fake million dollar smile. The reason he didn't include Kane in his plan: the douche-bag couldn't be trusted. Terry's attempts to avoid Kane knowing of the climb failed. Either way, the trek stayed on.

He trudged through the rocky, snow-packed path between the tents and stopped short at the sound of coughing hammering from one of the tents. He found his buddy's tent and leaned in: "Hey Lefty, you okay in there? Or do you need a little mouth-to-mouth?"

"I'm fine, just some phlegm."

"You haven't said much since we left for ABC; mind if I come in?" Terry asked.

"Sure, if you can stand the mess. I fired the maid."

Terry hunched, sitting next to his friend. Lefty's pale blue eyes remained focused on the roof of the tent as he stroked his almost white-blond hair. Lefty didn't smoke or drink, and yet crow's feet ingrained his impressionable skin. The mild temple balding added insult to injury. Lefty's downhill looks weren't caused by the recent turn of events torturing him, but a lifelong habit of vexation.

"Alright, what the hell's bugging you?" Terry asked, laying his head against a back pack.

"I told you, just a little phl—" Terry stared at Lefty. "You know what the *hell* has been bugging me: this whole *fucking* trip."

"You wanted to go on this climb as badly as any of us, why—"

13

"That was before leaving the company. I can't even send Melissa a letter to let her know I'm alive," Lefty said, his voice cracking slightly.

"We've been over this, Left. Once the trip is done, and the world thinks we're dead, we can go back for Melissa."

"Terry, she thinks I'm dead! Melissa knew about the threats and the "accidents" before we took off."

"You told her? It doesn't matter; it was either disappear or end up like the others," Terry said, trying to maintain a smooth tone.

"We should have let her in on the trip," Lefty said, rubbing his chest.

"It's safer this way." Lefty looked with disbelief at Terry. "Look, I'm aware that Melissa climbed with you before, but she has never passed 17,000 feet. She *might* have handled it."

"She could have stayed at Base Camp," Lefty said, forcing the words out over congestion.

"And how would she come with us over the summit? We're not coming back to the North side, so how does that work? It's safer this—"

"*Safer*?" Lefty interrupted. "Going up a mountain that chews climbers up like candy is *safer*?" He stopped with a coughing fit. "But you're right about climbing over the summit. She might have made it; Melissa is tougher than you give her credit for."

"Maybe. I know this isn't the vacation we planned before all of this, but it's our chance to—"

"Bullshit!" Lefty cut in. "You have a ticket out of this mess; you're here for the climb." Lefty stared unblinking into Terry's eyes.

Terry tried to hide the sting of the words. "The summit is a dream of mine, but the group comes first."

"Ter, I'm not concerned about getting down, I'm okay with dying on the mountain." Lefty paused, looking down at his hands. "I bet you think that's stupid."

"Yes, it's *very* fucking stupid. What about Melissa?" Lefty's head snapped up. "You just said—"

"Stop right there, don't..." Lefty stopped himself from yelling. "I have a package I want you to deliver to her when you make it down. A journal that I have written in since everything started." Lefty held the parcel out.

"I don't want it; you're giving it to her yourself."

"It's my life, my call. I'm here and there's no changing the fact that if the company were to get word that we're still alive, they'll hunt us down like all the others. Melissa is safe for now; I want it to stay that way."

Terry scooted out of Lefty's tent. "Have fun planning your death."

"Always so fucking high and mighty. Pompous prick." Lefty ended on a long series of hacking.

Terry kept walking away from Lefty's tent as the words faded. The air seemed thinner than earlier; the soup Terry ate for breakfast threatened to come back with a vengeance.

"TERRY!" Topher Gibson came running over, panting for air. "We have a big problem. It's Davis. He's still sick," Topher said, bracing his hands on his knees, sweat threading through the light brown-stubble on his head.

"Great, just what we fucking need," Terry said, rubbing his face.

They bolted for the mess tent, more of a jog given the lack of air. Terry swatted at the opened door flaps, and Davis lay, sprawled motionless on a makeshift cot. Terry leaned toward Davis' pale face, obscured by dirty blond hair. An eye popped open: "Wh-what're you looking at?" Davis said in a horse voice.

"You passed out, Davy," Topher said, stepping to the other side of the cot. "Let's get you up."

17

"I got a little light-headed. Waking up to a couple of dudes staring at me isn't my idea of a good time," Davis said, sitting down in a camping chair.

"Davy has been sick since we left Base Camp; he said it's just a small bug, that it would pass after some medication."

"Hey, whisky is medication. Apparently doesn't work on what I got. No biggie, in a group of docs I'm sure I'll be fine. And I won't try to ascend if I don't improve."

"Might want to leave the whisky," Terry said, taking notice of a small greenish fiber protruding from Davis' skin. "Hey Davy, what's that poking out of your hand?"

"Um, a splinter?" Davis said.

Terry grabbed a pair of tweezers from his fanny-pack, along with a sample container. "Whatever it is, I'm plucking it out to test later."

"Ter, how are you going to test it without a lab?" Topher asked.

"I'll figure that out later. Let's get Davy back to his tent."

Chapter Two

"God! Yes!" Laying flat on his back, Davis stretched his legs, pain-free. "Yeah *baby,* Davy's back!"

"Sounds like someone is having a good time in there without me. Should I be jealous?" A thick feminine Russian accent said.

Footsteps crunched snow-packed rocks as they approached; the shadow of a curvy form stopped at Davis' tent. The zipper door parted and a woman with long, blonde hair stepped in.

"You're the last woman to worry yourself over jealousy, cara mia." Davis sat up as the woman knelt down.

"I'm not Italian," she said.

"Yes, my dear Aglaya, I know." He lifted her fleece jacket to do the same to her shirt and kissed her stomach.

She moaned; it came out as a frisky growl. "You must be better; I like."

"My dear, this damn illness has kept me from enjoying you, but today I'm *back*, and ready to consume you." His grin made her breathe deep, her cheeks flush.

Aglaya pushed on his shoulders, forcing him back. She crawled on top of him, kissing her way to his lips. His hands rubbed down her back and he rolled her over taking the top position.

"My little secret, how are you, my love?" Davis said.

"I'm great now, but I tire of being a secret," she said in a sultry tone.

Davis kissed her deep, stopping only to say: "I know, Aglaya, but it's better this way."

After an hour-long unbridled ride of bliss, a sudden spike of pain jolted from the base of his neck, ran down his spine and curved around his body, throbbing through his chest. Worse than the leg cramp he had

had during the last round he'd spent with Aglaya. Davis wanted to give her at least two hours of ecstasy before stopping for the night.

"*Ohhhhhhhh...*" he grunted.

"Shhhh, not so loud; you're getting away," Aglaya whispered.

His cock still inside of her, he froze and fell on top of her.

"Baby, you're not done yet. I still need—"

Davis leaned up, clenching his chest. He mouthed words, but to no avail.

"Davy, what's wrong baby?" Her voice was panicked.

She uncoupled and flipped Davis over onto his back. His face wrenched as if something fought its way out of his body.

"Davy!" she said, slapping his cheek. "What's wrong, baby?"

Davis clutched at his chest, miming his inability to talk.

"Talk to me!"

*

The following morning, the texture of a soft face rested on Davis' slow-breathing chest. The utopian bliss he had been lusting for since meeting Aglaya, now a reality. Her arm lay slumped over his stomach.

"Aglaya?" he whispered to himself.

They agreed she wouldn't stay the night of the climb. Sunlight threatened to expose her leaving the tent, but damn, she looked so peaceful sleeping.

So soothing to watch her sleep; another first in their relationship. Davis could see himself lying next to her in the morning every day. He caught himself from taking the idea of marriage any further.

After his third and last failed marriage, he'd sworn off doing it again. Three strikes, he was out. But then he'd met Aglaya; beautiful, untamable, and damn, a fucking *goddess*. In that moment, the mental imagery of the two of them growing closer, and spending their lives aging in union, rejected his apprehension.

Aglaya awoke with a smile, her eyes entranced in his. "Are you feeling better, my love?" She kissed his chest.

"What do you mean?" he asked.

"Last night..." Her brow scrunched. "You were in a lot of pain."

"I don't remember that."

"I'm glad you're better now. Though it happened before we could..." She drew out the last word, tracing a fingernail across his growing shaft. "Finish."

With a devilish grin, she climbed on top of him, pressing her lips in several firm pecks along his neck. He ran his hands over her ass, squeezing her cheeks. He may have forgotten all about last night, but he would remember today for many reasons. The last

reason, the one he could have done without: a strange smell. It wasn't the scent of their juices mixing from last night, but something disgusting, something...
dead.

*

"God... my stomach..."

Davis jerked awake the next night as his abdomen contorted. His muscles twisted, knotted into a ball of pain right beneath his solar plexus. The passage of time blurred, his innards felt like they were being stirred with a wooden spoon, leaving sharp splinters in his organs. Struggling to breathe, he worked his lungs hard to stay alive. Still at 21,000 feet above sea level, his body reacted to the high climate as if it was 26,000 feet. The familiar stench of death filled his nose.

"Hey Davy, are you sure about trying to make it to Camp Three?" his friend, James Giovanni, said.

"Nothing is going to—" He stopped for a coughing fit. "Stop me from making this climb. I-I just need a little more time to acclimatize."

James, always the pretty-boy scientist; the type that drew women in with his dimpled smile before wooing them into bed once they'd discovered he was a big-wig micro-biologist. Dubbed *Frat Boy* by his friends, they compared him to Dick Clark; the cursed perpetual teenage lust to the ladies. James could be insufferably annoying, but loved his friends. Unless a woman flashed a smile his way; then he would drop his comrades in a minute. Davis kept Aglaya a secret in case James tried to steal her away.

"Alright, buddy. Just not a good idea climbing the mountain sick. The plan is to get back down, not die up there...well not *literally*. You can't do it on your hands and knees."

Does he know about me and Aglaya? Davis' mind became temporarily numb to the pain, and shifted to paranoia. *Fucking prick, I bet he's fishing for information.*

"I'm not going to sit—" Davis coughed, slinging gobs of saliva through the air, showering James' arm.

"Davy, man, cover your fucking mouth," James said, reaching for a bandanna. "Not to sound insensitive but I don't want what you have."

That's what you get for wearing a tee shirt, dumbass. Davis' mind went back to numb clarity.

James, accustomed to low temperatures, took it for granted. Davis buried his mouth in the pit of his elbow as another coughing storm erupted.

"I'm telling you, Davy, you shouldn't climb. Stay here, recover, have some soup and some tea. When you're better, climb down and we'll figure out another-*ouch*."

A strange pricking sensation distracted James. He threw the bandanna into his Ziplock bag, and scrubbed the area with a sanitized pad. The unknown prick stabbed through the cotton pad; some kind of splinter, too small to clearly make out.

Unable to argue, Davis doubled over. Fighting to stand, one arm around his stomach, he kept the other over his mouth. His throat stripped bare before the coughing subsided. Taking advantage of this brief lapse, Davis ran straight into his tent.

Sliding head-first on top of his sleeping bag, he left the tent door unzipped. He held his face over a small pail and, without hesitation, the last few meals came back with a vengeance, like a scene from The Exorcist. James returned with a towel and sanitizer spray. Spritzing down the doorway, he called out to Davis:

"I'm going to inform Terry that you're out of the climb, at least for the first round. We still have two months before the weather goes back to unclimbable. But to be honest, you shouldn't even attempt. I know you won't take no for an answer. Just think it over."

Dominated by his abdominal muscles, Davis locked his face over the pail. He wanted to flip James off, but couldn't move his hand away from clutching the side of the bucket. The smell of death incensed his need to vomit; then it turned into taste, like he'd bitten down on a fresh corpse. His stomach retched harder, tighter, fiercely sucking the life out of him. The plan to reach the summit became a vague thought; the taste of death made him hungry. The smell filled his tent.

*

Five hours with the insufferable sensation of bugs crawling beneath his skin made Davis fear moving. Frozen in his bedroll, he pondered if he could muster just enough strength to stab the buggers. It would tear up his body, but it would be worth it. Completely drained from the coughing and vomiting, his plan of assault appeared hopeless. Whatever plagued him seemed different than a normal flu bug. His fingers started to twitch; commands to make them stop were futile. His toes followed, increasing with life of their own.

"Hey Davy, how you doing?" Terry Marshall asked, popping his head in the doorway.

"U-um, w-well, I'm better. Sorta. The coughing and puking have stopped," Davis meekly replied.

"That's good, Davy, real good. Hey listen, I don't think you should summit. If you improve in time, then you can try to go up with the second group, though you will have to descend down the South side on your own and meet up with us."

"I-I know... I don't even know if-if I can—" Davis stopped as tears pooled.

Lefty Craven poked his head in: "It's okay, Davy. You don't have to talk. Just stay here and rest. We'll figure this out."

"I-I... ohhh... what's the word? Um... I can go up when—" Davis struggled to speak.

"Don't waste your strength, man. We'll get you down somehow," Terry said.

"I feel like I have... *Alzheimer's*..." Davis said followed by a weak chuckle.

"And it's on that note you're staying here. Stay course, brother," Terry said, kneeling down by Davis and clasping his hand.

"Don't worry Ter. I'll keep an eye on him. If Davy can't make it, I'll take him back down and meet up with you at the location," Topher Gibson said from behind Terry.

"F-fuck, guys. I'm not, not wanting to drag you down. You s-shouldn't babysit me."

"I'm just going to stick around and make sure you don't get worse," Topher said. "I have some meds in the first-aid kit that might help. Before we left our lives behind I stocked up on all kinds of antibiotics, and—"

"I won't be responsible for you n-not summiting."

"I plan on reaching the top, just not on this round." Topher stroked his blond stubble, peering over Terry's shoulder. "And we need another one of us in group two. The original plan is meant for us to travel in group one."

"Agreed," Terry said. "We have a new plan, and it's sound. Group one will be heading out in the morning. Take care guys."

*

Davis passed out after sunset. His dreams made less sense than normal. Darkness of overwhelming damnation; the profuse feeling that enriched his mind. The imagery could have been a sunny blissful day and it would still have carried the anxious distress like a million kiloton weight.

The time when Davis climbed K2 sprung to mind. He almost didn't make it back down alive; over 28,000 feet above sea level, he'd summited and made it back down without a touch of altitude sickness. So why did 21,000 here on Everest torment him?

The dreams shuffled through various adventures of the past, different mountains that looked like foothills compared to the one he was crippled on now. Every challenge he'd conquered.

Now he stood on the summit of Everest. A feat he had yet to achieve. But there he stood before the glorious sun that electrified the carpet of clouds, penetrated by smaller peaks. He felt like a god, but the thick sensation of damnation swelled inside.

His paled to the point of looking dead. The smell of death returned as he tried to walk toward the path leading down the South Side. But rigor had set in. The other climbers looked at him like some monster created in a lab. Sharp fibrous splinters protruded from his skin, smothering his hands with infectious spines.

One climber started to run as Davis grabbed him, the hands grappling, the spines digging in. The climber scream and Davis tore out his throat.

With the taste of blood and flesh, Davis awoke, breathing hard enough to rival an Olympic runner. His sleeping bag squished from sweat, his mouth and throat dry from dehydration. His fingers fumbled at the lid of his canteen, failing to unscrew the cap. It flew off at last, and he threw back his head, chugging every drop. *Empty.* He must have drunk it in his sleep. No one else could have, or maybe someone *did*; one of the other climbers sabotaging him for some reason? Maybe one of his closest friends was really on the payroll of the people that wanted him dead; or maybe he was deluded from the virus.

Searching the darkness he found a water bottle. *Empty too.* He fumbled around for his head-lamp; he slid the strap over his forehead and switched it on. His sleeping bag was littered in green and black fibers. He started to stand. His body ached as if it had been struck by a wrecking ball. It took every bit of energy to crawl on his knees. Every water bottle he found: *empty.*

"Everything okay in there, Davy?" Topher's voice pierced through the tent walls and tore through Davis' head, causing a massive migraine.

"Ah... yeah... I can't find any water... so damn *thirsty.*"

"Did you drink it all?"

"What the hell is that suppose to mean?" Davis said, his eyes narrowing.

"Nothing, man. Here." Topher tossed a bottle in to Davis. "This will do for now. I'll get you some more."

"Thanks." He tried to sound sincere.

Tightness formed in Davis' throat and chest, like a knee pressing down on his ribcage. His fingers and toes had stopped twitching, but now they felt like hot pokers. Dizziness swept over him, and he collapsed onto his bed-roll, face-diving into his pillow.

Even with his eyes closed, he could feel the tent spinning. His cheeks burned; his pelvis ached to the point he fought back tears. No refuge from his damnation. The smell of death increased in potency.

Topher returned with a couple bottles of water when he saw Davis hugging his pillow.

"To-Fu, is that you?" Davis asked.

"Yeah buddy, I'm here, and I have water."

"Are my eyes open?" Davis rolled over. "I can't see a damn thing."

"Um, yeah."

"I closed them for a minute, and then when I opened them I couldn't tell." Davis waved his hands in front of his face.

"Okay, Davy, I'm going to help you with the water, just stay calm."

"I'm not a... a... child." His throat tightened further.

"I know, Davy, just let me—"

"*Get away from me!*" Davis shouted, clawing at thin air.

"Alright, alright." Topher started to hand the bottle over to Davis. "Here's the fucking water."

Davis wildly snagged one of the bottles from Topher's grasp, feeling the mouth of the bottle with his lips. "Just calm down, man."

"Get the hell out of my tent... someone has been drinking my water while I-I sleep."

"No one has been in your tent, Davy."

Davis chugged the entire bottle then threw it at Topher.

"G-g-get away..." Davis stopped, trying to gather the words. "F-from me..." His voice reduced to a low raspy tone. He hugged himself to limit the uncontrollable shaking.

"Okay Davy, okay. I'm leaving; you're going to pull through this."

*

Animalistic cries of agony kept Topher awake all through the night. Screams of lost souls from the bowels of hell fluttered to mind. He had had enough and jumped out of his cot.

"*Davis*?!?" Topher unzipped Davis' tent and saw his friend holding the left side of his stomach as he cried out in pain. "What's wrong now?"

"M-m-m-my are, h-hurting... I think I'm passing a stone."

"Now you have kidney stones? We need to get you off of this mountain, *now.*" Topher pressed both palms against his head trying to think.

"I can't move... it'll hurt m-more. J-just get me some water."

"As long as you don't flip out on me again."

"Please... get me o-*out* of here." Davis said, pushing himself up with one hand.

"You think you can push past the pain?"

"I-I think s-so..."

Chapter Three

Sitting back in defeat inside Lefty's tent, sweat slid down Terry Marshall's chilled skin. He watched as Lefty tried to revive James Giovanni.

"I can't feel a pulse..." Lefty said as wind pelted the tent. "*One... two... three four... five...*" Lefty's close-cropped hair clung to his pate. He fought to get air into James' lungs. Between the lack of oxygen at such high altitude, and the immense panic, Lefty gave up.

Taking what little breath he had, he forced a few words out: "T-Terry, I need you... to breathe into the Os mask."

Terry grabbed an oxygen mask and placed it over James' mouth. Two hundred mile-an-hour gales pounded against the thin walls of the three-man tent as James lay motionless on Lefty's sleeping bag. Terry didn't have much air to give, but he seemed to handle the altitude better than the others.

"*One... two... three... four... five...*" Between Terry and Lefty, they tried four times to revive James. A streak of sweat defied the rigid cold, stretching down Terry's forehead and plummeting onto James' cheek. Thunderous clarity brought reality home: James wasn't coming back. Terry slumped back in the tent and stared with glazed eyes. The sound of those words stuck in his head.

"I don't understand." Terry sat motionless, forcing himself to speak. "He hasn't been sick, no signs of edema. He just... just stopped breathing. H-he just *stopped...*"

"Could have been anything; maybe an aneurysm," Lefty said, wiping his face. "With this altitude it could've triggered one if he was already susceptible."

Lefty stepped out of the tent, utilizing the rain fly as a harbor against the massive force of wind.

Terry stared out through the small window from the open door taking in the scenery. Neighboring peaks poked through the cloud floor in a blurry landscape. He'd never felt so small or insignificant.

*

The low oxygen at 27,390 feet above sea level riddled Lefty's mind and body. How much of his waning mental ability was resultant of James' death? One in four climbers die every year on Everest, and James had gone without any signs of a problem. The shit they'd all run from; it was no doubt their former project catching up with them. What junk did they get exposed to in the lab before leaving?

Cold, ferocious wind slammed against Lefty's face; the tent offered only so much protection. His eyes fixated on the dark sky, and then his sight shifted to the summit. Fuck dying here. Can't cheat fate; might as well try for the top. The entire group had made a pact to summit, especially if any of them died on the trek. After this, he would live his life as a hermit. James would have wanted him to live, at least long enough to enjoy summiting. Not much inspiration for Lefty, but the notion of the summit changed that for the time being.

Too many good friends had died. James was the first death since running; all of the others for what they knew. Lefty could never put the paranoia behind him as the others did, the thought that they were still being followed. The men they worked for weren't stupid, and they could find anyone. Terry made a great leader, and had done an amazing job at raising everyone's morale. Seeing Terry taken aback, falling into the same fear that had driven them out of their former lives, Lefty felt weak. Maybe he should lighten up a bit on Terry.

Another dead scientist on the list; one less whistleblower for the company to worry about. That made James number seven. So many pointless deaths. Damn...

*

The sun slowly peeked over the snow-packed rocky ridges of Everest as Terry unzipped his tent and stretched. The loss of James still fresh on his mind, images of his lips blowing through the filter on his oxygen mask. The lifelessness in James' eyes overshadowed the pristine vision of the scenery. Lefty calling off the count as Terry's hands pumped this friend's chest.

Terry took a long sip of hot coffee, watching the Sherpas bury James in the ground. One of the few spots without snow, the best they dug a small indention, covering the top of James with rocks. He also served as a distraction to the people hunting them. An unaccounted body for them to chase.

*

Unable to stop coughing, Lefty Craven pressed against his ribs, bracing them. Sleep ignored Lefty. He took sleeping pills, indifferent to the stupidity. Only three pills, just to be safe.

"Lefty?" Terry yelled in to him. "You alive in there?"

"That's to-be-announced."

Terry slid into Lefty's tent. "Hang in there, brother. We aren't at the summit yet," Terry said, placing his hand on Lefty's shoulder.

"Not even to the Death Zone, and already you have summit fever," Lefty said, stifling a cough.

"I know you're ready to die here, but I was hoping you might have—"

"Yes I want to summit, but that's where I get off. I'm done, Ter. I love you, like a brother. I'm sorry I haven't be a friend lately. I miss her, Terry. I wake up at night with tears frozen to my cheeks because I know I'll never see her again. And it kills me to think she'll run into those bastards from the company. I'm not able to save her. I can't be there for her. All I can do is cough my ass off on a rock, thinking about her as she tries to forget about me. I'm dying and she thinks I'm already *dead*."

"I'm sorry too, Left. If I could have, I would have brought her along."

"You should have," Lefty said, followed by a short coughing burst.

"It's not safe—"

"Exactly. Not safe, but she's not safe alone at home while I go climb a fucking mountain." Lefty's voice stripped as it started to rise. "At least here we could be together. We could hold each other. I'd get to die in her arms instead of pretending to be in them as I lay here alone. You know what I get to hug? My pack. It's not her, and it sure as hell doesn't *smell* like her. All I can smell is this strange stench of decay."

"Left, you know this isn't about climbing some stupid rock in the middle of nowhere. This is where we disappear doing something that everyone knew we'd dreamed of. When the company's wet-works goons come looking, this is where our trail ends. My head's off the chopping block, but the rest of you are still on their radar, and—" Terry paused. "Decay? What do you mean?"

"When we started out, it was a faint odor. But ever since James died, the smell has increased in intensity. I can taste it on my tongue."

"I have noticed something similar. I figured it was an aftertaste from one of those God awful space-bars," Terry said.

"I think there's something inside of us; something we created together," Lefty said.

"We never finished the project." Terry cocked an eyebrow.

"No, but we did enough. The company didn't have any problems killing us off. If we weren't done, they would've let the others live until completion. What we created pleased the company, and we outlived our usefulness."

"There has to be more to it. We would have seen something in the results if there—"

"Not necessarily, Ter. The others who were killed off, they worked on it, too. And I don't remember seeing the end product before we took off. The company could have had another team finish up. We don't even know the official name of our former employers. Who knows what else they were up to."

"If we're infected, we need to find somewhere to run tests. I know a few—"

"Wouldn't do any good. I'm not sure if this will kill us, or if it will mutate, but I bet the only way to stop it is through the same lab it was born in. If we could find the others who worked on this...but they could be dead too, or on the run," Lefty said.

"I don't know about this shit, Left, but we got to finish what we started."

"I just need some sleep. My mind is starting to play trucks on me; I think the pills are kicking in." Lefty rubbed his face.

"Get some rest. We're climbing this mountain together, and we're getting down together."

*

Standing outside of his tent, Terry stared down the path he had climbed. The beauty of the landscape overtook the sense of danger. The mountain itself seemed like a small oyster to worry about; the company, a tiny frog of a mud puddle. Terry built his career on doing the impossible; he'd use that to get him and his friends out of this shit. Taking a sip of black tea, Terry noticed a small green fiber sticking out his finger; a strange looking splinter in this habitat. The smell of death filled his nose, consuming the flavor of his tea. Either Terry had contracted what Lefty had, or it was James, haunting him.

Everest should be the only thing to fear; the rock that kills one in four climbers a year. Terry chortled at the notion. He plucked the splinter and pretended the taste and smell of death didn't exist. In his head he switched subjects. The sun shone through the clouds; mist swallowed the neighboring peaks. The landscape made it so easy to forget everything. Then the smell increased and the sight of James' lifeless body, his pale skin and absent heartbeat, stole Terry away from la-la land.

*

Doubled over, Aglaya stood at the opposite end of the camp. The trace amount of food she'd managed to ingest covered the snow-packed rocks on the ground. Her throat was stripped raw, and the thought of early edema had already occurred to her.

Stubborn like Davis, she forced herself to stand straight.

Fuck, I shouldn't have left him.

With all the climbers in the night, it wouldn't have taken much to miss him in the crowd. The heavy clothing and snow goggles made everyone look the same. Assuming Davis wasn't stuck at Advanced Base Camp. *At ABC dying... shut up!*

She flicked on her head-lamp, exposing blood splatter on the ground. Various strange looking fibers were mixed in with it. In shock, Aglaya backed up without thinking. She tripped over a tent line; sliding

51

against the nylon texture she struck the cold, hard ground.

"Aglaya, you okay?" Terry Marshall's voice came out of the darkness.

"Uhh, I'm fine...just...a little light-headed from the altitude. I'll be better once I get back to my tent."

"You need to get back on your feet first," Terry said, helping her up.

Aglaya completely forgot about Davis; her brain churned like a branch in the middle of the ocean.

Terry guided her into the tent and she cautiously slid on top of her sleeping bag. The tiny bit of relief turned to panic as she heard a slight snagging sound against the surface of the sleeping bag. Her hand: the source of the snag. Focusing her eyes, tiny black and green fibers protruded from her skin. Identical to the fibers smothered in the bloody vomit. As a microbiologist she saw things that were the bane of nightmares; this was new.

"Are you sure you're okay?" Terry asked, perplexed.

"Um, yeah. I just think I-I got a splinter somehow. I'll be fine, just need some rest."

"Okay, yell if you need anything," he said, leaving.

Quickly, she grabbed her fingernail clippers and tried to snip the fibers off. Instead they came out pretty easy. They were like cacti spines. After plucking several, dizziness overtook her and she passed out.

The next morning when she woke, memories of the previous night were a blur. Like a long night of drinking. Stretching her arms, aside from slight stiffness, she felt great. She rubbed her neck and immediately felt a prick. Pulling back her hand, more fibers stuck to her palm. The memories came flooding back.

She crawled out of her tent, cautious where she placed her hand, and returned to the blood spot. Standing over ground zero, she stared in horrid revelation at the blood-stained vomit, salted with fibers.

Is this what Davis has? Did he give this to me? Or did I give it to him?

*

Davis being sick off and on for weeks, Lefty not doing much better, and Aglaya joining in following James' death, made a nice shit-storm to wade through. It might have been from the altitude for most of the calamity, but that didn't stop the virus from being less of a threat.

A rock shifted nearby, yanking Terry from his train of thought. Not uncommon on a mountain, just a bit close for comfort. He scanned over the site; the only loose rocks he could see were the ones covering James' grave. The rocks hadn't moved; his mind was over-reacting to the nothing.

Terry went back to his self-chastisement as more rocks rustled. He refused to look back; his consciousness added insult to injury.

The smell of death was particularly bad that morning.

Chapter Four

"I'm alive after all!" Michael Davis stretched his body in various directions. "Fuck me, this feels great!"

He unzipped his tent and stood staring at the majestic view of the sunrise. The day had arrived to head for the camp at the North Col.

"Excuse me, sir, but do you know where I can find a sick and belligerent man? His name is Michael Davis, and—" Topher said, smiling.

"Funny guy. I'm cured, doc, so tread softly. I just might pull a few UFC swings on your ass."

"Speaking of which, we haven't had the chance to watch the last fight." Topher said, sipping on his tea.

"I know. I think maybe the illness was withdrawals," Davis said, stretching his arms as high above his head as his muscles would allow. "Oh well, we can watch it on the website when we get back."

"You're lucky, Davy. Today is the last group going up."

"I guess it's just meant to be, *mon ami*," Davis said, delivering a powerful slap to Topher's back.

"Hey Davy," the medical doctor, Miles Jensen, said. "Mind if I give you a look over before you pack?"

"I suppose not, though nothing, and I *mean* nothing, is going to stop me from the climb."

"Of course," Miles said, with perky bedside manner.

*

Wind blew harder as the temperature dropped. Terry's group pushed on up the narrow path, only a few yards away from camp. They trudged past a dead climber with his remains half-wrapped in a tent. Those who died on the mountain stayed on the mountain, which didn't matter to Terry. The elements held such low priority in comparison to the unknown illness devouring his mates.

After a while, the path narrowed further, leaving no room for more than a single-file. It curved around the mountainside, and the cave named after a dead climber who still lay there, Green Boots, came into view. It served as a vivid reminder of the dangers.

Terry heard a cough from one of the climbers, and he remembered Davis. The other climber threatened to cough up his innards. It was difficult to think that Davis probably wouldn't make it on the descent.

Michael Davis, one of the best microbiologists Terry knew, and an even better friend. It sounded like Terry was planning Davis' eulogy with that train of thought.

What if the company knew they were on the mountain, and had an assassin already on Everest? The urgency of following the trek down the other-side drove Terry harder, but knowing that his blood could mean, not just his death, but the death of others, almost persuaded him to side with Lefty on opting out.

James had had it easy. He'd died quickly and hadn't had to deal with life as a weapon of mass destruction.

Chapter Five

"Davy, you ready?" Topher Gibson asked, unzipping Davis' tent.

"Yeah... hold on," Davis said.

"What's wrong, buddy?"

"Nothing. Almost ready."

Topher slid his head inside. "I'd hope so. We're an hour behind, and we have to get going to make the North Col in time."

"Okay, Tofu, I'm finishing up my gear now."

"Seriously, what's wrong?" Topher asked, picking up Davis' pack.

"*Nothing.* I just had a rough morning. It's almost impossible eating anything at this altitude."

"Ain't that the truth. So is that all? Just a little altitude sickness?" Topher asked.

"I'm good, though. Had some black tea with a bowl of Ramen noodles. It will have to do."

"Hey Davis, mind if I look you over before you leave?" Doctor Miles Jensen said as Davis followed Topher out of the tent.

"*Thanks,* Tofu, like I need a doctor now." Davis turned his attention to the doctor. "I'm fine, doc. Nothing more than what the others are going through at this altitude."

"Good to hear, but I'm going around giving everyone a check-up," Miles said, pointing with an open palm for Davis to sit in a camp chair. "I've already treated three climbers; one sun-burnt the roof of his mouth. That's what happens when you ignore my warning against breathing with your mouth open on the climb. Then, a Chinese climber found face first in the snow with cerebral edema. And then—"

"I get it, doc. I meant that I'm no worse for wear. I tossed a few cookies earlier, but I'm holding food down now." The smell of death intoxicated the air; Davis readjusted his focus. "I felt like I was running up stairs with a plastic bag over my head, but I'm breathing better now." The scent met his taste-buds; he licked his lips without thought.

"Your lips are dry?"

"Ah-yeah, a little, but I have chapstick in my bag." Davis' stomach growled.

"Topher tells me you had a bad bout of coughing during the night. He said it sounded as if you were hacking up something big enough to ride," Miles said, moving his stethoscope across Davis' chest.

Davis turned to Topher with a glare. "I had a rough night. I didn't break anything, so I'm good."

"Just looking at you, I'd agree. But that's just from a cosmetic point-of-view. I can't stop you from climbing; just don't be afraid to come back down if you can't make the summit."

"No worries, doc, my *mommy*," Davis looked at Topher with a cocked eyebrow, "will be with me every step of the way."

Topher said something, but the taste and smell of death had Davis' full attention. His stomach growled loud enough to make Miles a little apprehensive.

"Davy? Did you hear me? I said I'm sorry, man, I—"

"Yes, Toph, I know. One day it feels like I'm a beach, the very next it's the fucking North Pole. Of course I'm going to be off my game a little; who the hell isn't?" The smell driving him mad intensified.

As he stood up, his legs buckled. "Oh shit, you okay Davy?" Topher asked as he and Miles grabbed their faltering colleague.

"I'm good. My legs just went numb. Let me sit here for a bit," Davis said.

"You really shouldn't sit in the snow; the frostbite—"

"I'm good, doc."

Topher and Miles lifted Davis to his feet. "We can still turn back," Topher said.

"God, what is it with you pussies? I said I'm fine. The numbness is from sitting too long; my legs went to sleep. I need to get moving to keep my circulation." The scent watered Davis' mouth. Topher's neck looked delicious.

"What do you think, Miles? Turn back?"

"I'd say it would be a good idea, though with the shit you guys are running from, this may be your best chance. Up to you guys. If you do go up, take care of each other. I have to treat a couple more patients. Have a safe climb."

Miles headed for another tent as Topher stared at his sick friend. "Well, Davy, maybe we should continue on. I just don't like the idea of you collapsing on the path."

"Is it any worse than dealing with the company?" Davis said, straightening.

"You got a point there; I can't argue."

"You shouldn't try to argue with me in the *first* place."

"Whoa, looks like you're feeling better after all. Nice 'tude, sailor."

"It's going to be this 'tude that keeps me climbing. Don't count me out yet."

Chapter Six

The wind howled as Terry Marshall and Lefty Craven clung to each other. The dark walls of cloud were barely below them, like a monstrous Lovecraftian *thing* edging towards them for the next meal. Relief filled Terry's mind as the sun shone down on top of the blackness. For a moment, it cast a silver lining over the ominous anxiety.

"We made it!" Terry said, fighting to breath.

"Of course we did," Lefty said with less air in his own lungs. "Climbing a mountain isn't like rocket science. I barely passed that subject in college."

"The others should be up soon."

"Assuming that the storm hasn't blown them off the mountain," Lefty said, staring off at the consuming abyss swallowing the neighboring peaks.

"Aren't you a ray o' sunshine."

"What sunshine? I don't know, Ter. We lost one friend already, Davis might be dead, and we haven't dealt with the company yet. What if... what if we panicked and left our lives for *nothing*?"

"There you again with that defeatist attitude," Terry said. "No one else is going to die; we're going to make this together. There's no room for doubt. That's what gets a person killed." Terry sat down in the snow next to Lefty.

"The plan is shot all to hell. Let's just enjoy the sight, and die in dignity."

"Fuck's sake, enough with the dying shit. We're—"

"You're my friend, one of the best, but you don't get to tell me what to think or feel. We're done, Ter. There's no getting off this mountain. What happened to James, what's happening to Davis, it's going to happen to us all. I can still smell something rotten, like something died in my nose. I can taste it. This isn't natural; it's whatever we were working on. We're *infected*."

"I know," Terry said as he slid his mask off and rubbed his face.

"You-when?"

"As soon as Davis got sick, my gut tightened, like it does every time I know something isn't right. The very same feeling I got when the shit started hitting the fan at the company, before we found out," Terry said.

"That damn gut of yours; I know better than to argue with it." Lefty massaged his numbing hand. "And what does your spidey-gut tell you about trusting criminals to hook us up with new lives?"

"Uncertain."

"At least you're honest." Lefty smacked a hand against his knee.

"What's wrong with your hand?"

"I'm losing feeling. The damn cold is getting to me almost as fast as this damn infection." Lefty stopped short, concentrating on his breathing.

Terry stood, stretching for the sky, taking in a huge gulp of the minute amount of air it offered.

"Hey, kid. Care to give me a hand?" Ronald Kane asked, standing on top of the Hilary Step, just below the summit.

Terry applauded.

"I'd clap too, if I could feel my hands."

"Oh funny," Kane said.

Terry sauntered over to the edge and reached down.

"It's about time, old man. I was about to order a pizza, maybe download a movie from Netflix. Thank God I didn't have to break down and pull out my last Snickers," Terry said.

"Listen to you talk about food. I haven't eaten all day, and that's if you count an energy bar that tasted like bat-shit," Kane joked as he panted for air. "Which is nothing more than a stick of some fancy-named crap that hardly lives up to its reputation."

Ronald stopped and braced his hands against his knees. "We've a problem. Aglaya is sick."

"Not surprised." Terry scrunched his brow.

"She started showing signs back at Camp Four, but she has been getting increasingly worse." Kane took a big swallow from his canteen. "My money is on cerebral edema. Aglaya doesn't seem to know where she is at times; she has been very snippy, and claims that the other climbers are plotting her death, just like with the others who were murdered."

"Where's she now?" Terry disregarded Aglaya's paranoia; it was obvious where it came from.

"Stuck back at the Second Step."

"Well, nothing like saving a crazed friend on a hundred-foot wall with a ten-thousand-foot drop-off to make things interesting," Terry said with a sigh.

"You planning on going back down the North Side?" Kane asked.

"Yup, don't have a choice."

"The odds of you making it up, and down the South side, aren't good. You know that, right?" Kane asked as he unpacked his paraglider.

"Never tell me the odds. My trip as been forfeited. I'm going down to scoop up Davy and Aglaya. Do you think you can forget the glide down, and take Lefty to Southside Base Camp?" Terry asked.

"No can-do, Capt' Solo. My trip down is set in stone. Maybe one of the other—"

"No worries, I'll go down with Mister Science God," Lefty interrupted.

"C'mon now, Left, you need—"

"Don't tell me what I need; I was kidding about that god part." Lefty stood, shaking.

"Well then, you two old ladies got it figured out." Kane motioned for Terry to lean in. "Listen, if you're

71

the last man standing, and you think you might not be able to make it back down, there's an extra glider in my tent at Camp Three. My Sherpa was supposed to use it but changed his mind, and he's heading back down once the storm passes. So the glider is yours."

"Where's your Sherpa?" Terry inquired.

"Sick. Not too bad, but after what happened to Davis, he didn't want to risk it," Kane said, avoiding eye contact.

"Alrighty. Have a good flight." Terry slid back into his pack.

"As much as I hate to be the realist," Lefty said. "how the hell are you going to get three sick climbers off the mountain, and fake our deaths?"

"I'll cook something up for the deaths, but getting you guys down is the trick, and I haven't got that far yet. But we will get there."

"Good Lord, Ter, your optimism kills me. I don't know which is worse, that or this freaking illness. But hell, I can't let you take the credit for surviving this beast alone, and I'm sure as hell not going to die without seeing you make it off of this rock."

"You old softy." Terry lowered himself onto the step.

"I'll show you old—" Lefty erupted into another coughing fit.

"Tough talk. Take it easy following me; you're not allowed to die."

The coughing let up. "There you go again, telling me when I can die."

The radio crackled as Topher's voice broke through.

"TERRY!"

"I'm here."

"Davis is getting worse; he's coughing up something I've never seen before. He needs off of the mountain, and *soon*. I'm taking him down."

"Careful, Tufu, the storm is coming in fast," Terry said.

"I see it. The damn thing is coming for us. We're heading toward Camp Four."

"Good luck, brother."

*

Eight hundred and some odd miles from Camp Four, and Davis was fading fast. Stuck on the Northern Ridge, he lay face-down in the snow. Still conscious, he coughed up more of the fiber-salted blood. The signs of pulmonary edema terrified Topher. Davis could barely move, leaving Topher to unclip from the fixed rope so that he could guide Davis into Green Boots' Cave. Covering Davis in a blanket, he removed Davis' goggles and hat, feeling his forehead. Davis was burning up. Topher shoved a thermometer into his friend's mouth and held him still.

The wind surged stronger than it had all week. Peeking out from the cave, Topher's innards coiled at the sight of the vast sky, a floor of damnation. Pitch-black clouds obscured all visibility of the miniature landscape below. With the storm below, another cell moved in at eye-level.

Topher took the thermometer from Davis' mouth; it read a hundred and fifteen. He should be dead, but for some reason he hung on. Perhaps the edema was somehow keeping him alive.

Davis coughed harder, projecting fiber-laced splatter all over the frozen corpse of Green Boots. He moaned between each spasm; the muscle twitches were bad enough Topher could see them.

"Hey... Tofu, I think I got something a little worse than edema," Davis fought through his stripped throat.

"You're delusional. We're going to get you down, and you'll recover. Just hold on."

"When we were back at the lab, and Steven died in that *accident—*" Davis struggled to get the words out.

"Hey Davy, not here, not *now*. That wasn't your fault and you know it," Topher said, winching at the trashing wind.

"What I'm saying is, he was just a lab-assistant. And somehow he accidently dropped a vial he didn't have access to. Steven wouldn't break the rules; hell, he followed the rules better than anyone. And the damn vial wasn't found in the lab; it was in the janitor closet," Davis said.

"What are you getting at?"

"Going on the run, we didn't do it because of Steven. Everyone but me bought it that he'd fucked up. Just another victim targeted. He knew something. And if he *did* break the rules by stealing one of those vials, he did it to expose the company. None of us knew what he had; it came from another department, but with this shit inside of me I can only guess what he had." Davis took slow, deep breaths.

"Maybe, but right now you need to rest." Topher adjusted Davis' blanket.

"That storm hits, no one is resting."

The electrified cloud floor flashed out of sync, a living carpet with a voracious hunger. Thunder slammed into the mountain with a fist of divine wrath. Davis held himself as he coughed blood. Unrelenting, Topher gave up offering words of encouragement.

He tried to hold Davis in place to keep him from hurting himself.

"Oh God, my-my throat is raw. My fuckin' ribs, I think I broke one." Davis coughed again sending a chunk of blood into the air; it splattered Topher across the face. "Shit, Tofu, I'm sorry, man."

Topher wiped the blood away; as he did, he pricked his finger on something. Pulling his hand back he saw fibers in the blood.

"That's it. We're getting the hell of this rock." Topher grabbed his radio.

"Aye, Tofu. Tell Scotty to beam us up and to be sure to have a bottle of brandy waiting."

*

"Immense pain is a good thing, right?" Lefty Craven asked, massaging his hands through the super-thick gloves. "I guess I haven't lost all sensation yet. We need to get down; walking in this wind is only going to speed up the frostbite."

"Don't worry; we're well on our way back." Terry's optimism faded as the view of the Second Step came into view. "Oh shit." Lefty stopped in shock at Terry's defeated tone. "A bunch of them are just hanging on the Step."

"*What?*" Lefty peeked over the edge.

"Hey, guys, what's the hold up?" Terry yelled down.

No response. He continued to yell until one of the climbers replied.

"A climber isn't moving. I think she's sick."

*

"Okay, Davy, c'mon," Topher said, swinging Davis' arm around his neck.

"Yeah—" Davis coughed up more fiber-infested blood. He made another attempt to talk. "And perhaps I can grow wings and fly us down to Base Camp. Any luck raising Enterprise?"

"If you can grow wings, I'd like to know why you haven't done so by now. And I think Scotty finished off that brandy; we're on our own."

"Enjoying the view, and the air is so nice up here, what there is of it."

"Actually, there's a lot of air, just not the kind we need. Higher amount of ozone. Too bad it's deadly."

"I'm a bit slow, but did you say something about alky?" Davis said with a grunt to indicate a laugh. "Why's no one sharing? I'm going to raise holy hell! Fuckin' engineers."

"Yeah, when we get down you're getting some medical attention."

"Are you kidding? I'm in the company of doctors."

"None of us are medical doctors; the best we can do is figure out what it is you have based on a sample," Topher said as the smell of decay made him want to gag.

"If you take me to a hospital, our names will be recorded and we'll be flagged. I need a Scotch." Davis felt the urge to cough, but couldn't.

"We'll figure it out when we get down, and I didn't bring the Scotch."

"Tofu, you need to leave me here. Just go on without me." Davis' tone changed.

"What?"

"I'm not just a liability, but if I'm contagious, it would—" Davis went limp.

Topher couldn't handle Davis' weight and dropped him in the snow. He tried to keep the fall from injuring Davis. Topher barely handled the exhaustion.

"Don't quit on me, Davy. *Wake up!* Come on!" Topher's yelling was trumped by his voice cracking.

He sliced through Davis' clothing with a knife, not taking into account how this would guarantee his friend's death, even if Davis pulled through. Pressing his mouth against the oxygen mask, he pumped Davis' chest. No breathing. No heartbeat. After a couple of tries Davis coughed; it was the hardest fit he had yet suffered.

Still no pulse.

Topher removed the mask. Davis spewed blood, smothering Topher's face.

*

"She's not responding," the climber from below said. "We need to get her down. There are climbers trying to descend. This woman could get us all killed."

"Jeff, are you saying she's not breathing?" his friend asked.

"Just light breathing, that's it." Jeff rubbed his neck. "Her skin is pale. We need to unhook her and take her down."

"Dude, we're halfway up the Step. Are you fuckin' serious?"

"Shut up, man. She's saying something under her breath; it sounds German or Russian."

*

Terry Marshall tired of waiting. "We're coming down, make room," he yelled.

Lefty moved to the ladder; one of the other climbers scooted aside at the base, allowing room for Lefty to squeeze through.

"I'm going to unhook briefly. Hang onto me," Jeff said.

"Dude," his friend said, staring off at the ten-thousand-foot view below.

"I know man; just don't let go."

Terry carefully climbed down the small ladder passing through the bottle-neck of protruding rocks. Jeff stood aside as Lefty continued on, stopping as he passed the sick woman. The words were in a Russian accent and recognizable: Agalaya.

Lefty forced some words out; her eyes were closed, tense. He tapped her on the cheek and her eyes shot open. They held a grayish tint, and green fibers stuck out from the sclera.

Speechless, Lefty watched Aglaya's face contort from confusion to rampage. Jeff lost his footing.

"Man you gotta go. I need back onto the rope," Jeff said.

Lefty had to move on, his mind a dark chamber of dense fog; the harder he tried to think the more his became soup.

Terry started to pass as Jeff again unclipped, letting out a sigh with a clear tone of annoyance. Terry noticed Aglaya's face. She growled as he placed her goggles and mask back. He checked her oxygen tank gauge, the needle frozen in place.

"C'mon already, I need to clip in. We'll take her down," Jeff said.

"How? It's impossible to carry anyone down. Better off getting her conscious and having her move." As Terry spoke, he knew from her eyes Aglaya would soon be gone.

"Yeah, just as soon as you get the hell out of my way, that's the plan," Jeff said.

Too exhausted to argue, Terry started back down. "Alright, when you get her down, my friend and I will take her the rest of the way."

*

"Hey I think she stopped breathing." Forgetting to clip onto the rope, Jeff removed her mask. "We need an oxygen tank STAT. I think she depleted the other one."

"Man, you know none of us have extra O's."

"I barely have enough air in my lungs for myself; I don't think I can revive her." Jeff looked her over and spotted green and black fibers stabbing out from her cheeks. "What the *hell*?"

Jeff took off his glove and slightly raked his fingertip over the fibers. One slid into his skin. Jeff gave up on the woman, and started to hook back onto the rope when she woke up. Her mouth opened followed by a hiss; her tongue a blanket of fibers. Saliva strung between her teeth, petrifying Jeff.

Her head lunged forward, snapping at his neck. A near miss, Jeff slipped and fell off the Step. Snapping in all directions she aimed with wild abandon for any piece of meat she could reach. With what little air they had left, the other climbers screamed. One of them reached over with a knife and sawed through the rope. Her footing lost, she tumbled down the hundred-foot rock face.

*

Aglaya struck the rocks below the Second Step, slamming into the ground. She staggered to her feet and glared up at the climbers who had denied her a meal. Lefty didn't stop. Still hooked onto a different rope, and dangling above her, he had to get past his deranged friend. Terry followed suit.

One of the other climbers hung at the base of the Step only inches away from Aglaya. Clawing at her face, she ripped the goggles off and jerked her face up. The sheer madness of her expression made it clear that *no one* would pass.

The climber unhooked and jumped on top of her. He dug an ice ax into her shoulder. She kicked him off. For someone who had just died she still remembered how to fight; at least on an instinctual level.

Standing, he brought up the ax. She charged at him causing him to miss. A line-drive propelled him into the air. The climber fell backwards in a football tackle. His screams echoed throughout the mountainside as she tore into him.

Lefty refused to stop. He let the pull of gravity hasten his descent to the ground. He couldn't move very fast once on the ground, but Aglaya, oblivious to his presence, gifted him the time to slide by.

Terry landed on the ground, stopping at the sight of the climber's blood as it soaked the snow around his body. Terry jerked his head up; he couldn't lose Lefty.

*

Topher scrubbed at the blood frozen to his skin. The smell of death made his throat gag. It wouldn't stop. The smell of the dead overwhelmed his senses. He dry-retched; the innards weren't ready to paint the snow.

Davis' dead body shot up fast. Too fast for someone in perfect health, and way too fast for a dead guy. Davis staggered a little, clutching his stomach.

Topher removed his goggles, catching sight of his friend's eyes. Davis used to have brown eyes; the iris was now black, the pupil a pearl white. The sclera a grayish-green.

Davis looked bewildered. He twitched his head, taking in the surroundings. Reddy-black blood trickled from his mouth. The atrocious smell trumped the scent of decay; an amalgamation of burnt piss and maggots.

Topher backed up. Davis sniffed the air. With a snap of his head he took notice of his old friend; looked at him like a meal. Davis' lips twitched like an animal about to attack.

Topher made the futile effort to jog away, but Davis charged. Not a single plume of breath escaped his mouth. He grabbed Topher, shoving him down; sinking his teeth into Topher's neck he pulled back a mouthful of nylon fabric.

Throwing weak jabs, Topher fought with no air in his lungs. No strength, no sound to cry out.

Finally able to reach his knife, Topher rammed the blade into Davis' kidney with no effect. Stabbing Davis dozens of times, Topher remained on the bottom.

An open opportunity, he thrust the knife into Davis's eye-socket. With a loud groan, Topher pushed him off, sending Davis of kilter. He grabbed the small shovel from his pack and bashed Davis' face in.

Blood erupted from Davis' mouth in a surprise coughing fit. Fibers peppered the red puke. His mind grew fuzzy before clearing once again; a swinging light in a dark room. Not stopping, Topher took the extra rope from his pack and tied up Davis. Black, cloudy circles pocked Davis' face with red and black fibers growing from the center of the swollen areas.

With the final knot tied, Davis shot up, pushing his shoulder into Topher's chest. Davis ran like a cheetah through the snow-packed path. An uncontrollable madman.

What the hell went wrong with Davis was beyond Topher's understanding. He'd gone from living, to dead, back to living as a crazed cannibal. Like something from a Dean Koontz novel.

He walked as fast as his body would allow toward Green Boots' Cave. Collapsing, he met the snow face-first. He queried the possibility that Davis would get frostbite in his condition, what with being dead and all. Silly thoughts; Davis was dead and Topher would soon join him. And that damn scent, that fucking smell of *death*, if he had the strength it would drive him mad, but his dying body already guaranteed that.

Everything fucked. All of them had worked on the same project, developing new genes and bacteria material for the specialized 3D printer lab. Creating what they were told was biological augmentation against illness and bio-terrorism. The genes that would save mankind; the crap-speech Dr. Kane gave at the inaugural meeting.

Ribs ached as another cough tore through his lungs, prying his jaws open. The onslaught burst through his mouth. A hundred-mile-an-hour wind whipped into the cave opening. Topher clung to the ground, embracing himself to prevent his body from tearing itself apart. Curled in the fetal position, Topher projected more fiber-blood, carpeting the snow. After witnessing Davis' plight, and now his own, he knew that the bug they had created was mutating.

Wind tingled along his spine; chilled shockwaves tickled his guts. With coat zipped, goggles covering his eyes, and his hands gloved, the frigidity toyed with Topher. Chilled and hot pinpricks swept through his entire body. His insides churned; fibers penetrated his skin.

A dynamic voice roared in his head: "Fuck this mountain and fuck this virus... fuck *me*!"

All the raspy declarations weren't going to improve his situation. With those final words, Topher took a deep breath, and shakily clambered to his feet for one last trek off the mountain—

—only to be knocked on his ass by a huge gust of wind.

Chapter Seven

Exhausted from treating frostbite all damn day, Miles Jensen's vision played tricks on his mind. The lack of oxygen exacerbated his weakening state. So far none of the climbers were going to lose any limbs, or any other various body parts for that matter.

Alright, self. I can't put it off anymore. You hear me? You're just going to have to suck it up. We have shit to do, fingers to save. Let's get this trip over with. Miles gave himself an internal pep-talk.

He headed to his tent, and on a whim glanced over at James' grave; the rocks that were the mound lay flat. One of the climbers must have thought they were funny disturbing the site, though most of the climbers had spent too much money on the trip to run the risk of being banned from the climb. Miles shone his head-lamp over James' grave; empty.

The smell was like maggots and stagnant water with a hint of burnt piss. Miles buried his mouth in his arm, yet still the scent made its way to Miles' tongue. All the time he'd spent around dead bodies in the past, it had never smelled like this.

He looked around for anything else out of place, but found nothing. His head-lamp scanned over a set of freshly shuffled footprints leading out of the camp. Following the path he came close to entering the Dead Zone. Going any further without an oxygen tank would be suicide. He headed back to camp to grab a tank.

Almost back to his tent he saw Dex Danner. The only person on the climb Miles could see doing something stupid, like messing with a grave. Even that was highly unlikely. Dexter thought it would be cool to use the slang term, Dexamethasone, as his official name. It was rumored he'd even changed it legally. The man lived for the climb as much as any other mountaineer; he didn't let his unnatural size stop him.

An ape. That was the image that sprung to Miles' mind. Dex was a biker with hair long enough to braid ropes for the climb. Scruffy-bearded and smothered in so much tattoo ink it was impossible to know where one tat ended and another began. He was also a self-professed prepper, just waiting for the inevitable zombie apocalypse. Dex was dubbed a walking miracle after surviving a nasty motorcycle accident, and one more miracle to add: the fact that he'd made it this far on the climb.

"Hey, Doc-man, do you ever sleep?" Dex asked, unzipping his fly to piss next to his neighbor's tent.

"Ugh, I don't think anyone sleeps at this altitude. So what's up with the grave over there? Yesterday it was covered, now the rocks are scattered," Miles said, trying to avoid eye-contact as Dex fire-hosed the ground.

"Good question. I figured varmints got him." Dex shook a few times and zipped back up.

"You noticed the body was gone and you didn't bother to tell anyone?" Miles asked.

"Didn't figure it would matter; damn varmints. Good luck trying to find them up here. You feel me?"

"There are animals up this high above sea-level."

"Oh, well maybe it was one of the other climbers tripping Bath Salts. That shit turns ya into a zombie, ya know?" Dex buried his face into the collar of his coat.

"You should have said something."

"Not my problem. My name's Paul, and it's between y'all," Dex said, stepping toward his tent.

"Okay, Paul," Miles said, turning away.

"A funny doc; good thing to have in a climate like this. A good bedside manner is the best medicine, I always say. "

Ignoring Dex, Miles grabbed his oxygen tank and secured it to his body. After a little ways, Miles made it to the Exit Cracks, threading himself through the huge rock. It was here that he gave up; the odds of anyone getting this far with a body slumped over their shoulder were astronomical.

Miles looked over the shuffled footprints and figured the climber was a druggie; it didn't seem like they'd lifted their feet as they walked. The footprints turned into hand prints, as if someone had tried to climb the slope on their hands and knees. Something that looked like thread was scattered and stuck in the prints. None of the prints appeared to be made by a gloved hand; someone didn't care about frostbite.

This person had broken obvious rules of climbing, and somehow had the strength and breathing ability to lift a two-hundred-pound body and carry it. Or had they had been carrying James? Crawling up the mountainside would mean they'd have to have tossed James' body somewhere.

Among the howling wind a different sound broke through the thin air. A strange moaning. Difficult for Miles to pinpoint, it was time to head back to camp. As he started to turn back, a human head fell from the sky and bounced on the rocks next to Miles. Miles jumped back, losing his footing.

Dangling on the rope, he toed the rocky incline to reestablish his footing. He stepped back onto the ledge, checking in the direction from which the head had fallen. Suddenly, the head appeared in the beam of Miles' head-lamp.

"Dear God!"

The severed head rolled off the ledge. A moan came from the darkness above; the direction from which the head came. The half-decayed face of James

Giovanni craned into Miles' light. James was alive, sort of. *Alive?* Maybe a ghoul now. Bones sliced through decrepit fingertips, barbing onto the ledge above. His eyes focused, jaw wide open, saliva stringing between disgusting teeth as it started to freeze. The slavering jaw snapped like a dog biting at steak.

Miles stared, open-mouthed, questioning how James could be dead and still able to live, still able to move. His posture, though awkward, still manageable. Miles cranked his O's and went back to descending.

The dead man clawed after him. Stretching further, James slipped. The fall didn't faze James; he fought to grab a hold of anything that promised food.

James grasped for Miles' coat; slipping, Miles again found himself dangling from the rope.

Reaching out for the nearest rock, James clung to his back. Regardless of impending death, the creature that was James snapped at Miles' neck. Swinging like a pendulum, Miles cried out for help, which went unheard in the wind.

James lost his grip, landing headfirst on one of the ledges below. His skull caved in; half-rotted brain-matter oozed out. This time James didn't get back up. Miles waited, knowing at any moment the thing that James had become could spring up, as it obviously had in the grave. When the oxygen from his tank ran low, Miles stopped waiting and aimed for the ledge.

*

Dex bit down on a pencil, sending tiny fractures through the processed wood. Two months before Everest, no cigarettes. Two months on the mountain, his big-bad-biker-dude persona wanted to die. Nerves rattled with anxiety; by now, quitting should be easy as eating pancakes. Leaving the smokes back home in a lock-box had kept him from slipping, but three patches a day wasn't working. His damn wind-proof lighter added insult to injury; a constant reminder of his oral fixation.

A juggernaut in extreme physical feats, there was nothing this six-foot-two, three hundred pound monument couldn't handle. The mountain itself paled in comparison. His addiction to nicotine was his Kryptonite.

The strenuous climb feebly attempted to bring him down, trying to kill him before reaching the summit. He'd fallen asleep in the snow at Crampon Point, which had landed him with Bronchitis, forcing him back to Base camp. The first barrage of strikes against the behemoth. Such poor odds made him beat every hurdle thrown at him. He rested now at Camp Three, right beneath the Death Zone.

Like a saucy vixen in a red dress, singing a sultry tune on a stage in some dim bar, the summit teased him, inflamed his fever for the top of the world. It toyed with him, even though he could taste the victory, could feel the high winds, and could soon bask in glory. He would be getting his picture taken for bragging rights to show off in his biker club. Better than sex while riding down the highway at sixty-five miles an hour. He was going to make the summit, even if he had to climb this monster half-dead.

A scream tore from the distance. It sounded like one of the climbers he knew. The altitude could destroy a man from within, but Dex had yet to hear anyone scream in agony. With frostbite, the usual sounds were moaning, crying, maybe a little whimpering, but no screams.

Something worse was on the mountain.

Dex started to investigate when the dark outline of something appeared in a neighbor's tent. Could the doc have been wrong about there not being animals on Everest? With a flick of his headlamp, the tent violently shook in the beam. The rummaging stopped with the screams. Only a few feet away from his own tent, where he'd left his ax; it might as well have been at the bottom of the Pacific Ocean.

Swallowing his fear, Dex envisioned himself as Vin Diesel and moved toward his neighbor's tent. The unzipped door-flap whipped in the wind. Peeking inside, the light flashed upon three other climbers, huddled over a man. Probably the one who had been screaming. The climbers appeared to be eating something; one lifted his head as a piece of flesh tore from the man.

It wasn't just meat, but an organ. The climbers were all gorging themselves on the man. They looked dead; their faces were uncovered, pale, and pocked with needles, or fibers of some kind.

Dex tried to talk, but instead mouthed: *what the fuck?* On auto-pilot, he stepped back, his foot slipping on a patch of ice, which sent the hulking biker flat on his back. Frantically struggling to stand up, he moved onto a fast crawl. En route to his tent, he craned his neck to find one of the cannibal climbers was in pursuit. It grabbed his foot, and he delivered a spiked kick to the climber's face. The man fell back, giving Dex time to get to his feet. Almost jogging, the thing chased him, keeping pace. Dex wondered who the hell could have slipped him a Mickey, because dead people don't run you down. If this was the beginning of the zombie apocalypse, it wasn't fair. His gun armory was gathering dust back at his home in LA.

Back at his tent, Dex was thankful for being lazy enough to leave the door unzipped. Jumping inside, he zipped the door shut just as pale fingers slid across the smooth fabric. The climber swung like a drunken ape at the tent, pounding for a way in.

Snatching his ice ax, Dex sat there, watching the bombardment of fists silhouetting the tent wall.

He couldn't laugh out loud; too anxious. But in his head he pondered the irony that the zombie outbreak he'd been warning everyone about had chosen now to occur. Out of all the places to start. Dex had been waiting for this, preparing for years. He grinned.

"Bring it on, formaldehyde-face," he mumbled. "Eat me, bitch. Ah, probably shouldn't have said that."

*

Miles Jenson made it back to camp. Pondering what story to cook up, he didn't waste time with the old, *"who's going to believe me"* cliché. With zombies on Everest, Miles would settle for playing stupid. James didn't seem like the movie ideal for a zombie, but damn close enough. What could spontaneously change a man? A *dead* man.

Walking past the first tent, a familiar moan came from inside. Another one of those *things*, maybe more. Perhaps a couple getting it on; they might have cranked the O's, popped a pill; crazier things have happened.

Holding the ice ax up, Miles approached the tent. *I'm going to feel a special kind of stupid if this is just a couple of climbers fucking... please just be fucking... what if it's zombies fucking? Can zombies fuck? Oh God, why did I have to think about that? It's the lack of air.*

An arm flew out of the tent; dark blue fingers covered in black and green fibers reached for him. Miles took off running, or at least he thought he was running. The dead man shot out of the tent and quickly gained on him.

The "zombie" grabbed Miles' collar with cold, strong fingers, hooking him like a fish. Miles grabbed for an ice ax one of the climbers must have dropped, and made his swing, allowing momentum to carry the blow. The zombie didn't notice his throat had been slit even as the oil-colored blood squirted from the gash.

Not deterred in his lust for Miles' flesh, the zombie stumbled, shoving Miles to the icy ground. A prickly hand grasped Miles's face—the fibers digging into his skin. Shoving the thing off, Miles buried the ax into the dead man's skull.

Back at his tent, Miles sealed himself in. A strange commotion caught his attention; he unzipped the small window by his bedroll, and saw four or five dead climbers straddling Dex's tent. A random breeze struck his flesh from behind. Snapping his head to the other side of the tent, he saw a hole in the fabric wall about the size of a half-dollar, no doubt from a scuffle between zombie and a living climber. *Fuck hiding.* Miles thought.

*

Sweat streaked down Dex's face; panic seared through his veins.

"Holy-fuck-shit-me!"

Zombies weren't supposed to be powerful maniacs; they were supposed to be slow, and weak. The ceiling thudded toward Dex as the tent-rods bowed from the pressure; the loops holding them began to rip. Dex reached for his ice ax as the roof partially caved in. Mouth imprints appeared in the fabric, dead, chomping jaws snapped at the tent wall, working to chew through. The fabric didn't take much to tear; a sharp bone from one of the zombies' arms sliced through, just missing Dex's leg.

"Holy sh—" The fabric tore further.

Dark blue fingers cupped the edge of the hole, ripping it further. Hands reach in as Dex yelled for help. He squirmed for the exit, fought with the zipper. As he slid his shoulders out, teeth chomped into his calf. He screamed. Halfway inside the tent, hunched over, the mob of the dead tore at Dex's legs, butting heads to claim their share.

Chapter Eight

Lefty's arm hooked around Terry's neck tighter as they approached Green Boots' cave. They gracelessly slammed their asses down onto the rocky snow. Lefty didn't bother to find out where on the mountain they were; his mind was a sluggish, murky mire. Terry slowed his breathing as the carpet of crimson registered. Gripping his ice ax, Terry used it to shove off the ground.

The now-infamous fibers were clinging to every surface in the cave. Terry held the ax like a baseball bat. Peeking around the rock bend, he spotted Topher, hunched.

"Hey, Tofu, where have you been?" Terry lowered his ax. "Found blood in the cave, and those fibers that

I have been seeing in everyone who's sick. Speaking of which, where's Davy?"

A rasp emerged from Topher; his head twitched to the side, staring down Terry. Lifting up slowly, he staggered after his new prey. Not quite as fast as Aglaya, but fast enough.

Bringing up his ax, Terry swung: "Sorry, buddy." With eyes and mouth closed tight, blood splattered Terry's face.

The body dropped with the ax still imbedded in its head. Terry tossed his gloves to the ground and wiped his face. The smell of decay traveled up his nose and down his throat. His stomach knotted up; vomit threatened to shoot out but only left him dry heaving.

Terry regained a shred of posture when he spotted Davis. Dark blue, fiber-spiked fingers stretched for Lefty's neck. Lefty swung weakly as Davis grabbed his wrist. Falling onto Lefty, his jaw repetitiously snapped. Terry tried to rush over but his legs had turned to rubber. He watched as Lefty tried desperately to fend off the monstrosity wearing the face of their former friend.

Terry's ax sliced through Davis' throat; he used the handle to spin Davis to the ground. Opening one eye, Lefty was transfixed by the blood dripping from his brow. Petrified, one drop seeped into his eye.

Davis chomped at the air; Terry's cleat-clad boot dominated his neck. One more blow. This time the ax buried deep into Davis' head.

Chapter Nine

Brilliant orange beams poked through the thin, white wispy clouds, streaking across Miles Jensen's face. Waking up twenty feet from the first tent of Camp Three, frostbite came to mind. At some point in the night he'd passed out. He held up his hands to check for frostbite; oddly enough his hands were safe. Much longer in the snow, and he might not have been so lucky.

Immersed in warmth, rejuvenation charged Miles with hope. With a shot of overestimation, Miles stood to finish his trek. His foot slipped on a patch of ice, and he crash-landed on his ass.

Worse. His feet were completely numb. His arm outstretched, he tried to reach his foot. *C'mon, don't do this to me!* The second push was the equivalent of grasping for the summit.

Third trip he clamped down on his toes. Picking his foot up, he dropped it, slamming it down repeatedly. Sharp pain spider-webbed through his foot.

After an hour of abuse, Miles stood, and fell. Keeping his hands flat, he maintained posture. No energy left, he slowly rose again. He entered the camp. His tent, the second from the last, faced him.

Thank God for small favors.

Arms, legs, moved like a zombie. *Am I one of them now? Whatever the hell they are.*

He fumbled at the zipper, and crawled inside. Taking off his gloves, boots and socks, he discovered that his feet were a pale blue. The tips of his toes had grown black. *It's sad when I can't tell the difference between frostbite, and turning into a zombie. Tell me God doesn't have a sense of humor.*

Firing up the mini-stove, he held his foot over the flame. The sensation of heat was absent. He reached over and switched his oxygen tank with a new one.

Cranking it to four liters a minute, he continued to wait for his foot to recognize heat.

Switching feet didn't yield success. The sound of climbers trudging by reached the the tent.

More summiteers.

"Wait! Stop! Don't go up the mountain…"

One of the climbers stopped to unzip the tent. "Are you talking to us?

"Yeah, there's someone up there trying to kill people. He's psychotic." Sounded better than the truth. "We need to get off this mountain."

"Right. Well we should probably check it out then. Who knows, maybe all of us can overpower one madman." The climber turned to his guide. "Apparently this guy has mountain sickness. Definitely cerebral edema. He's claiming there's a nut-job up the path trying to kill people. Even if it is true, I doubt he's dangerous in this climate. What do you think?"

"I'm sure the doctor will come to look in on him. The doc has been doing her rounds in the camp."

"Then we climb." The man turned to Miles. "Look, buddy, we're gonna take care of that killer guy. You just rest here."

"No! Don't go up there. You won't make it; you leave this camp, and you'll die."

"Promise ya, I won't let that happen."

The climber zipped the tent and headed up the path.

Miles continued trying to warm his feet, slapping them over and over, lowering them over the flame. Itching horribly, he reached up to scratch. His fingers raked over some sort of splinter, only these were growing out of his skin.

One splinter protruding from his neck stuck into his finger. Pulling his hand back, he was greeted by a green fiber.

More itching wracked his entire body. Even in places he didn't dare think about. Thousands of tiny splinters stuck out of his skin, catching on the fabric of his clothes. There was no hope of sliding into his sleeping bag to warm up with a chance of more sleep.

Miles broke out in a forceful cough that took all the air in his body; bloody deposits showered his tent. For a doctor this was something new. He couldn't treat himself with anything. Even if he saved his feet, he'd become one of those *things*.

After several coughing fits, it started to subside. His throat constricted, closing off his airway. The pinpricks fibers were growing in his throat now. His chest convulsed; his throat tightened further. He couldn't breathe, attempts were to no avail.

His foot dropped onto the stove without knocking it over, burning his heel as he lay there, motionless.

His eyes tingled in pain from the pinprick sensation. Miles couldn't move his burning foot.

Chapter Ten

"We made it, Left, we're out of the death zone, and past Camp Three. Not sure where all the dead fuckers went, but at least we are making it down," Terry Marshall said, entering Camp Three.

Lefty lifted his head a couple of inches. "Out? Mr. Optimist, it was called the death zone long before dead people ate the living. And judging by the blood everywhere, we're still very much in the death zone," he slurred.

"I don't see any of those things; doesn't mean they're gone, though. Rest in here, I will check the camp out," Terry said, maneuvering Lefty inside a tent.

Lefty slowly slipped into a sleeping bag as Terry zipped it.

Some of the tents were empty; others housed dead bodies that didn't move.

All of the walking dead people were gone. *Yep, walking dead people; that sure as hell makes sense.*

Going back to the tent, Terry lay beside him.

Rest, finally sweet Jesus, rest.

*

Terry woke up to moans, but with the hundred mile-an-hour wind, there was no way of telling what was what. He went back to sleep with thoughts of zombies, a blurred mess in his dreams.

The storm worsened outside, keeping the other climbers away. Terry heard the rumbling thunder and refused to let it keep him awake.

Two days passed before Terry awoke. All the memories of dead people gone for the time being.

Struggling to remember what had happened, the sight of someone's tent baffled him.

He struggled to his feet and crawled out. The sun was blinding at first; he slid on reflective snow-goggles. The view was priceless. Scanning over the area, he recognized it as Camp Three. He thought for sure he had summited. Walking around to stretch his legs, it all came flooding back. Only he and Lefty had survived.

His eyes panned over the site, stopping abruptly at the now empty grave of his late friend, James Giovanni. It wasn't just living people dying and then coming back. James had died for no apparent reason, and had been left in the ground for hours before Terry made for the summit. Possible that James had a mutated strain of the virus? If that was the case, it hadn't taken long to mutate.

It had happened. The illness that had swept through his friends, and it had to be the people he'd worked for. All members of the group had been in contact with the various diseases they were assigned to, but every one of them knew well enough to stay safe.

Revisiting the chain of events, for a long time, during their work, Terry had suspected foul play behind the deaths and disappearances of other scientists on the project. As things had got weirder, Terry started letting the others in on his gut feeling. After a few months of investigating in secret, and planning, they had decided to expose the groups that had hired them. But when people close to them had begun to die, they'd all decided on plan B: hiding.

Davis had got sick about the time they left. His illness lasted weeks. Now, within minutes, a person could get sick. Any one of the viruses that Terry and the others had engineered could be responsible for all of this. The science of the DNA they manipulated, the cross engineering, the cloning...

This sounded like something Lefty would say, but it made sense, at least in the oxygen-deprived brain of Terry Marshall. Hell, wasn't that the point? To make a super-bug powerful enough to wipe out an entire country? To die out quick enough to allow the invading army chance to set up shop? This was a test. Someone in the group did this to them. A controlled environment.

Time to get off the mountain. Terry could worry about remounting an investigation and attack against their former employers later.

He tried to wake Lefty, but his friend lay motionless. Lefty's hands were black. Terry cranked the oxygen, but it didn't stop the spread of frostbite. He grabbed a pack of self-heating hand warmers from one of the abandoned tents, and slid them into the gloves.

"Come on, buddy. Did you really think I was going to let you die on this rock? Melissa would kill me. Now get off of your ass."

Lefty's eye shakily opened.

"I-I-I wasn't gong to die without g-getting you down. Good ol' Ter, a-always the goddamn hero. I-I'll show you."

*

On their descent toward Camp Two, the bright color of fluorescent coats moved about slowly. Terry started to cry out, but stopped short when one of them staggered. On the mountain everyone staggers, but this was lifeless. They shambled in the same direction, like a horde, and were unaware of Terry and Lefty.

As the terrain became steeper, the zombies lost their footing and began sliding down the slope.

Lefty could barely focus on the excitement. Carefully, they marched down the slope as the zombies grabbed a hold of one of the fixed ropes.

Onward to Camp Two, Terry followed the dead, praying they didn't notice fresh meat.

*

Ten Hours Later...

Almost to the camp, and Terry stopped as the undead tripped over the tents, alerting others enough to come staggering out. Lefty kept walking; Terry tried to stop him, which was a big mistake as Lefty reacted with a loud, "*What?*"

Like starving children, the undead looked up. Standing in front of Lefty with his ax ready, Terry caught three Sherpas and a woman climber emerging from the tents out of the corner of his eye; after slamming his ax into the heads of the dead climbers, Terry lowered his weapon.

The woman had long and straight dark hair, and appeared to be living. Terry guided Lefty down and into the camp.

"I take it there's no doctor?" Terry asked, hoping for a positive answer.

"Um, 'fraid not," the woman said. "I-I'm Tia. These are my friends, Anil, and Sonam. They are the last of my group's Sherpas."

"My friend here has a bad case of mountain sickness, and his hands are frozen, literally," Terry said.

"The only thing we can do is get him off the mountain. Has he been bitten?" Tia said, eye-balling Lefty.

"Other than frostbite, he's fine."

"That's good. Set him down in that tent over there and I will fix you both some hot black tea. As long as we don't make too much noise, the dead-heads shouldn't bother us."

*

Three Hours Later...

The tent filled with steam as Terry boiled a pot of water. A huge crank of oxygen, and Lefty started to feel a little better.

"We have been taking O tanks off of the dead climbers; hasn't exactly proven to be easy. A lot of these zombies have been walking around anywhere from hours to days with the O's cranked. They just don't seem to notice. Most of the time the O's are all gone before we can reuse them, but we have managed to get a few partials. After we're done rejuvenating your friend here, we should be back to square one," Tia said.

"I do appreciate the help," Terry said, not taking his eyes off of his friend.

"Yeah, I figure we can make it down from here if we're careful. So it's not like I'm going to need the extra weight."

"H-how far did you make it before stopping?" Terry said, taking a sip of tea.

"This is it. I was down at the North Col, almost ready to leave for Camp Two, when one of the climbers made it back telling everyone that there were zombies up the trail. Those of us with the energy just laughed; the others looked at him like he was nuts. We just figured he'd come down with the sickness. So along with my group we came up here. By the time we made it, wouldn't you know a horde of fuckin' zombies. They looked fresh and they moved fast. Not like these malnourished ones."

"This virus has been changing rapidly. I've never seen a virus mutate so fast."

"Are you supposed to be some kind of egghead scientist?"

"I was."

"Oh, not anymore?" she said.

"Nope."

"What are the odds of something like this happening while you were here?"

"Astronomical." Terry finished his tea. "Are you sure that your Sherpas didn't get bitten?"

"Yes. We checked each other over," Tia said, clearing her throat.

"I meant after the zombie killing. I noticed that they got real close to those things."

"None of them got bitten. I'm sure."

*

"I know it's dark, but we should be leaving. I'm thinking these things don't see well at night," Tia said.

They packed up and headed towards the North Col. The two Sherpas helped Lefty by placing him in between them, and wrapping his arms around the back of their necks.

They made it halfway when Anil collapsed. Lefty fell on top; Sonam struggled to keep a hold of the climber.

Terry stopped, but Tia continued to walk ahead. Sonam fell to the ground. As Terry looked them over, he saw the green and black fibers sticking from their necks. He grabbed Lefty and checked his arms. The fibers didn't poke through the fabric.

He dug out his tweezers and plucked the fibers out of his friend's coat. Tia stopped.

She and Terry were pulling Lefty to his feet when the two Sherpas stopped breathing. Letting go of Lefty, Tia took her ice-ax and swung, hard, into the skull of each of them. Terry tried not to drop Lefty.

"Can't be too careful," Tia said, wiping blood from the blade.

Chapter Eleven

Terry took the lead down the mountainside. Lefty
trudged behind Tia, his mind starting to clear. The
fibers sticking out of Tia's coat were longer than the
others. Terry marched down the metal ladder that
bridged the gap of a chasm, using the ropes as
railings.

He stopped on the other side to catch his breath. Tia
started to walk across when Terry looked back at
Lefty, making sure was still alive.

Lefty removed his goggles and offered Terry a look
that suggested something very wrong, indeed. This
wasn't the look of mountain sickness.

Looking at Tia, Terry nodded his head; a clear signal
for Lefty to stop her. Lefty slowly moved toward her
as Terry stepped back onto the ladder.

Lifting his hands was the equivalent of juggling anvils. Regardless, Lefty fought the fatigue and numbness. By now, his hands resembled chunks of ice attached to his arms.

If Tia was infected, why hadn't she changed?

"What's wrong?" Tia stopped, confused by Terry's sudden behavior.

"We just need to check you over. Make sure you don't have any infections."

"*Now*?'

"Just let us have a look." Terry held out his hand, forcing her to stop.

"If you wanted to get fresh on me, it would have been smarter to do so back at the tent," she said, breathlessly. "Why on the ladder?"

"We just want to make sure you're not on your way to becoming one of those things."

"I get it. By keeping me over a huge chasm, you feel safe. It's in case I try to bite you." A pause; Terry didn't say a word. "If I *was* one of them, you would have already noticed. I would already be dead, and trying to eat you. Not talking to you."

"Just let us have a look," Terry said, losing patience.

"Us? Your friend isn't in any shape to be looking anyone over. You mean, *you.*"

Terry moved to within arms' reach of her as Lefty sidled up behind her.

"Unzip your coat so Lefty can check your neck."

"Lefty is in no condition to be doing *anything.*"

"Just humor us."

"Fine."

Tia ran the zipper down. Lefty tried to grab her collar without success. When he stepped closer for a better grip, she unleashed an elbow into his stomach. Terry reached for her as she swung her ax at him.

"Sorry, I'm not that kinda girl."

Lefty staggered towards her, and she stabbed with a back-thrust; the spike at the end of the ax-handle penetrated his coat, and bored into his stomach. It didn't go in deep, but enough to make him stop and favor his wound. With the other hand, she cut the ropes with a folder-knife.

"I told you, I'm not one of them," Tia said. "You couldn't just leave me alone. What am I? The only person infected who hasn't changed? These fucking splinters just keep growing out of my skin, driving me fucking nuts, but I don't *eat* people. I could have got help once we were down. But you couldn't let it go."

Terry maintained balance. "Tia, the reason you kept this from us is because you're a *carrier*. You had to know when the worst of the infection didn't hit. You saw what it did to your fellow climbers. You *know* how it works."

"Y-yeah. And you know what? I'm handling this climate better than *any* of you. The virus has made me stronger. For how long? I don't know. But long enough to get—"

Lefty wrapped his arms around her; sharp spikes from the crampon of her boot stabbed the bridge of his foot. She twisted her body and Lefty slid off.

Terry heard the cracking noise of Lefty's leg, the one tethering his friend to the ladder between the slats.

Lefty hung partially over the edge of the ladder. Tia kicked him in the face a couple of times, stopping only when Terry rushed up behind her.

She clawed to climb over Lefty; Terry repeatedly buried his ax into her leg.

The last blow he left in, and used the ax to hold onto her. With a failed kick from the other foot, she slipped.

Terry almost went with her as she wrapped an arm around the ladder frame. Her leg dangled at an odd angle.

The ax-cord around his wrist dug in. Struggling, he wiggled it out. The ax gave, sliding out of her leg. Tia disappeared into the darkness of the chasm, her screams echoing until an abrupt silence announced she'd hit the bottom.

Terry tried to pull Lefty up, but his friend was stuck.

"I know you don't want to hear it," Lefty said, calmly.

"Like that has ever stopped you."

"You remember when I said I wanted to die up here? Well it looks like I got my wish. Wasn't how I saw it in my head, but then, it never is, is it?"

"Fuck, Left, I wasn't going to let you have that wish."

"You may be a stubborn prick, but life has you beat," he said, chuckling weakly.

"You have me beat, and life is—" Deep moans interrupted their conversation.

Lefty lay back as far as he could and looked up the forty-five angle. Dead climbers were staggering toward them.

"I-I t-thought we k-k-killed them all," Lefty said, with a sigh of defeat.

"Apparently not."

"You know what you gotta do, T-Terry... you have t-to drop... the ladder into the chasm."

"NO! I'm not going to leave you. We have lost too many, I won't lose you, too."

"Ter–" Lefty was stopped by a coughing fit. "You don't have a choice. The edema, is starting, to set in... My hands are good as gone... and my leg's broken. You c-can't get me down. T-they are getting closer..."

"FUCK, Left, no. I've failed you, I've failed everyone. I can't, I have to save you. I just can't—"

The first zombie placed his foot awkwardly on the ladder edge until he attained some sort of balance. Terry charged back to the side facing the North Col. Completely on the ice, he stomped his crampons into the ground.

The first zombie slipped and fell into the frozen abyss, but three more crawled after Lefty.

"Those smart fucks. It won't be long till they get ol' Left. Sorry buddy..."

Highly unlikely the zombies would make it off the ladder, but just in case.

"Ter! Break. The. Fuckin'. Ice! Can't let these things get across..."

Terry chopped at the ice beneath the metal ladder until it broke free. As it scooted off of the cliff, the zombies followed it down into the deep void. Lefty, too, along with the dead. There came a muted crash.

Refusing to think about his friend, focusing solely on survival, Terry headed towards the North Col. He made it across another ladder, a straight shot over a V-shaped chasm. One foot on the other side, exhaustion finally forced him into submission.

Terry crashed into the ice-plated snow, planning to rest only for a few minutes. Before he could catch himself, his eyes had shut and the world was gone.

*

Growling.

The sound Terry Marshall kept hearing in his sleep, then another sound that he could only describe as tearing. As he opened his eyes, the sounds remained.

Down at his hands, a zombie gnawed at the fingertips of his glove, shaking its head spasmodically.

Terry jumped up, ramming his fist into the zombie's face.

The thing came at him. Terry clawed at it, trying to smash in its eye sockets.

His other hand landed on what he expected to be icy ground, but there was nothing there.

Terry fell backwards off of the ice cliff.

With his fingers now exposed to the cold, Terry held onto the ice edge, the ax dangling from his wrist.

The zombie reached for him; grotesque teeth bit down on his arm. Blood splattered across Terry's face.

The zombie slumped to the ground and, a second later, a Sherpa pulled an ice-ax out of its head.

He pulled Terry up to safety and sat him up with a fresh oxygen tank. After a while, the Sherpa led Terry back to the North Col.

*

Everything was normal again. A doctor looked Terry over, and cleared him to head back down to Advanced Base Camp. Just bronchitis, apparently. Terry stayed in his tent to heal up. The shit he'd suffered made this a cake-walk. His deep rest was disturbed by men in HAZMET suits, gathering everyone up.

"What's going on here?" one of the climbers asked.

"You need to come with us. This entire side of the mountain is under quarantine," a rifle-toting man in a HAZMAT suit said.

Terry had no choice but to go with them.

A bright light shone in his face, waking him up—again.

He was still in his tent, but not the one at ABC. He had awoke at the North Col. His mind taunted him with visions of his former employers, saturating his thoughts. The fog of high altitude cleared up, images of the dead walking now seemed to fit with his earlier paranoia. The only difference was how far *they* would go. The company hadn't appeared yet. That wouldn't last long. By the time the CDC made its move to quarantine the mountain, the company would already be spear-heading every step they made.

Fuck the descent. I'm going back up.

Chapter Twelve

The Sherpa that had rescued him, Adarsh, begged
Terry to go back down. The mountain was angry, and
the walking dead was a sign of its wrath. Even the
Sherpas didn't dare piss off the mountain.

"I understand," Terry said. "The way I look at it, the
mountain is already pissed at me. So I'm fucked either
way. This is my only chance; I'll take care of myself."

Terry shot himself with a double-dose of
dexamethasone which he found in his tent; very risky,
but not coming down with edema took priority.
Scavenging through the other abandoned tents, he
found a small metal case holding three needles of
DEX.

He stuffed two full tanks of oxygen into his pack,
and hooked a fresh one up to his chest.

I probably should tell Adarsh "thank you" one last time.

Geared up and ready, Terry started to hunt down Adarsh. He found the Sherpa petrified with fear.

"What's wrong?" Terry asked, but got no response. "Adarsh, what's *wrong*?" Terry brushed his fingers across Adrash's face.

Instead of talking, the Sherpa just pointed. Terry followed the path of Adarsh's finger. He was pointing at the path leading to the North Col. Difficult to count how many florescent coats had appeared, but all were worn by the dead, shambling up towards the camp.

"You might want to go to the summit with me. The South Side may be free of these things."

"These things, they come from Base Camp. I don't know how they made it so far, but odds are good they are on other side, too. You go, I stay."

Adarsh held up his ax, marching after the undead horde.

Again, Terry didn't look back, leaving the Sherpa to certain death.

*

It was one long haul to this point, not far from Camp Three. Terry nudged the valve on the oxygen tank. He tried to remember which tent contained the paraglider. Terry never did meet Tashi, Robert's Sherpa. Last he knew, Tashi was still at Camp Three.

Passing the outskirts of the camp, Terry remembered which tent. The open door-flap snapped in the wind. Terry peeked inside and found Tashi: dead. Robert hadn't mentioned his Sherpa not making it. If Tashi had died in the tent, Robert would have said something. *Wouldn't he?*

As Terry suspected, the paraglider was still there, on Tashi's side of the tent. He leaned over Tashi's body, half expecting the Sherpa to pop up and bite him on the neck. But instead, he discovered the man had a hunting knife wedged in his skull.

Robert, you bastard. You knew of these things, and failed to tell me? What the fucking hell?

He left his pack, and took the oxygen tanks off the body. Strapping the tanks to his chest, he slid the paraglider onto his back.

You didn't just know, you were the reason. Terry stared at Tashi, taking it all in. *You always did seem too cavalier about everything. James was cool because he drank himself to Utopia. You never had a vice, and yet you managed just fine. Too fine.*

Terry stood outside the tent, staring off into the skyline of the lower peaks. It looked more like Heaven than anything ever preached in church. Clouds made layered stories among the neighboring mountains. Bliss among carnage.

Enough of the Utopian escape.

Terry pulled out Lefty's wallet and looked at a picture of his best friend, and his wife, Melissa. They had been happy before this shit-storm. Of course, it wasn't his fault, but what if he'd left his friend to fend for himself? Sure, he and his wife would most likely be dead, but hell, at least they would have been together. Lefty was gone, leaving Melissa to survive on her own. The company would hunt her down.

Terry had to make it.

For her.

*

As he approached the summit, luck changed for Terry; the storms died down, leaving the window for a full haul up the path. The zombies had either fallen off the mountain, or frozen to its surface. But luck has a shelf life.

Terry hadn't paraglided from a mountain in ten years, not since his climb in the Rockies. Just like riding a bike, albeit in the air.

Once on the summit, he unpacked the sail, positioning it in front of him. The high wind started to pick it up as familiar moans trembled along on the air.

Terry looked back and saw a climber he didn't recognize lumbering towards him. This one looked a little different from the others. The fibers were now longer, and coated with a glossy surface. They poked through the fabric of the mountaineer's clothing.

The wind lifted the sail off the ground slightly as he tried to run. He cranked the oxygen tank up, and shot himself with another dose of DEX.

The zombie reached for his pant leg, and the fibers dug in. Its grip slipped as Terry lifted higher, but the damn thing left the colorful spikes embedded in him as a souvenir.

Terry avoided the idea of infection, and focused on the ascent. The slopes of Everest had never looked more elegant.

Hopefully, the zombies wouldn't last long on the mountain.

When Terry got back to civilization, he would phone in an anonymous call to the CDC, but he knew the company would already be there.

Chapter Thirteen

"This is Mister Kane, and I'm calling to inform you that the test was a success. By now, all the runaways will no longer be a problem. I told you, two birds, one stone. In a couple of weeks, I'll be ready for phase two of the test." Ronald Kane snapped his cell phone shut as he sat at a window-seat in a small restaurant in the town of Namche Bazaar.

The town rested on the steep side of a natural amphitheater in the hills. Though the houses looked dull, the small niche was actually quite lively. Kane enjoyed the cheerfulness of the quaint place. It made for a great contrast against his side gig. Who knew, if his little plan worked well enough, he just might move there permanently.

He took a bite of cake as he watched yipping dogs run through the streets. Tibetan ravens swarmed overhead with obnoxious cries. The sounds of goats and yaks added to the animalistic overture.

It was a nice distraction from his world. Kane took another bite of his cake just as the sight of a man paragliding caught his attention. The man looked like a climber. The coat, the goggles, the oxygen mask; Doctor Terry Marshall!

The fucker found the pack. He wasn't supposed to make it that far.

Terry landed in the middle of the street; townies watched, enraptured by his somewhat inelegant landing. Almost tripping over his own feet, Terry detached from the glider.

Doctor Kane took out his phone and hit redial. "This is mister Kane. We have a problem."

THE END

www.crowdedquarantine.co.uk

ALSO FROM

CROWDED QUARANTINE

THE WAY OF ALL FLESH

KEVIN WALSH

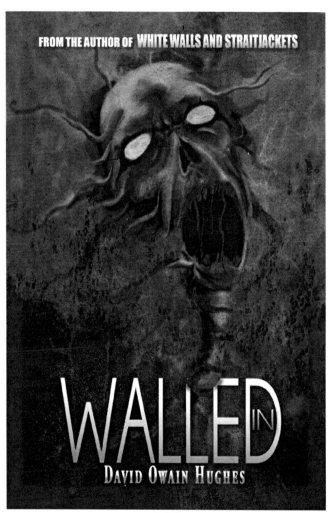

FROM THE AUTHOR OF **WHITE WALLS AND STRAITJACKETS**

WALLED IN

DAVID OWAIN HUGHES

152

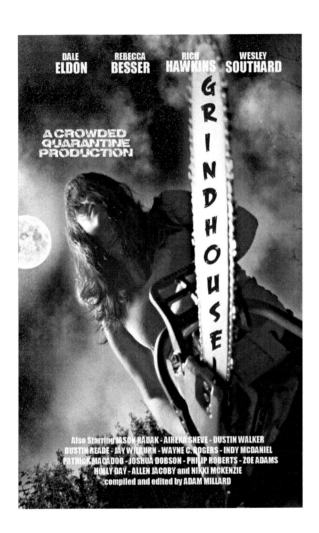

153

"Chilling as an Arctic blast, Craig Saunders' bold and distinctive voice will haunt your dreams." - Bill Hussey, author of *Through A Glass*

THE ESTATE

CRAIG SAUNDERS

"This is what Jack London would have written if he'd been raised on pop culture and werewolves... Exciting and taut" - Weston Ochse, author of SEAL Team 666

CRY WOLF

AURELIO RICO LOPEZ III